far away island

lake dog-a-bone

blue sky stage

"It's What You Believe Inside
That Makes you... *You!*
The Outside's Mostly
Fabrics & Stitching."

—Paddywhack Lane

Copyright © 2010 by Paddywhack Lane LLC. All rights reserved.
Published by Paddywhack Lane Press.
Paddywhack Lane Press is an imprint of Paddywhack Lane LLC., Parker, Colorado 80138 USA.
Paddywhack Lane is a registered trademark of Paddywhack Lane LLC. (USA)

www.paddywhacklane.com

ISBN 978-1-936169-00-9   10 9 8 7 6 5 4 3 2 1
First Edition
Printed in China.

The Costume Trunk Adventures™

Paddywhack Lane®

Lauren & the Leaky Pail

BOB FULLER

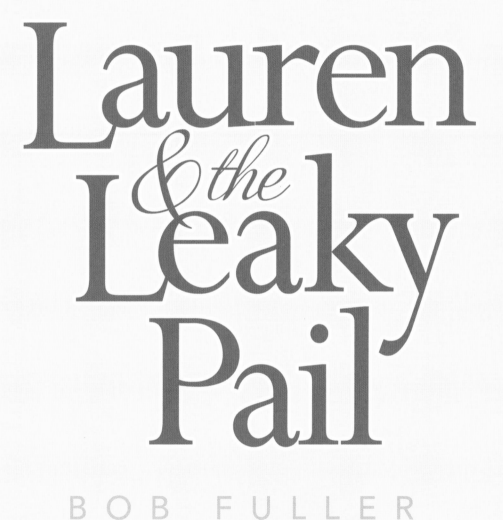

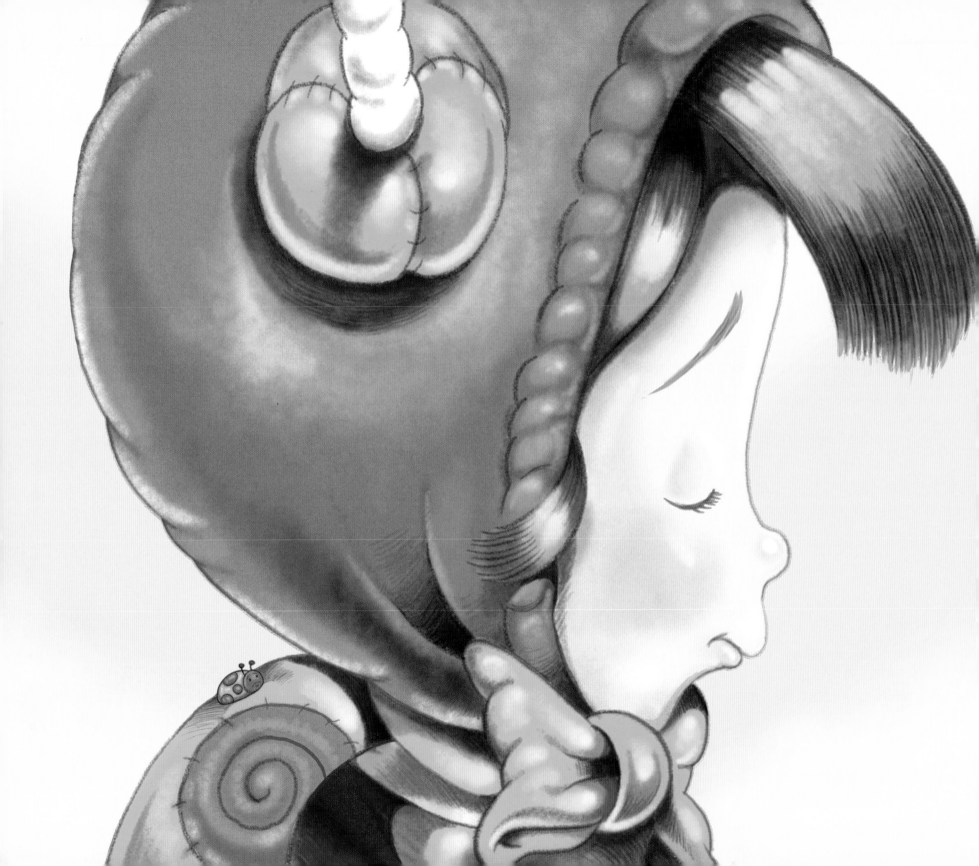

The Annual Fall Festival was only a few months away.

Everyone hoped to win first prize in the gardening contest.

No one hoped to win more than Lauren.

She had never won the gardening contest before.

In fact, she had never won *any* contest before.

Things didn't start well. Lauren offered to help clean up the clubhouse, while the other kids were busy choosing their seeds for the contest. By the time it was Lauren's time to choose, there was only one packet of seeds left.

"Brussel sprouts?"

"Yuck!"

Lauren picked up the seeds, and went to look for a watering pail.

YUMMY-GRO

BRUSSEL SPROUTS

Lauren peeked into the dark garden shed. "All of the watering cans are gone too!" Then, she saw an old pail under a bench. "I guess you'll have to do," she said. Lauren picked up the pail and headed to the lake to fill it with water.

While the other kids took a shortcut to the lake, Lauren chose a lonely, winding path through the hills. Lauren dipped her pail in the water and started back up the steep path to the garden. The pail was heavy and hard to carry. Water sloshed out the sides, and dripped from leaks in the bottom.

By the time Lauren got back to the garden, she was very tired. When she tipped the pail to water her seeds, only a few drops came out. Lauren looked at the holes in the bottom of her pail. "I guess I'll just have to make lots of trips to the lake with you," she said. "Then I'll get enough water for my seeds."

Lauren got up early the next morning. All day long, she carried her leaky pail up and down the dusty path from the lake to the garden. Each time Lauren reached the garden, she only had a tiny bit of water left.

But, Lauren didn't give up. She even shared some of her water with the smaller kids.

Lauren patiently poured water over her seeds. Little by little, they would get just what they needed.

One day, Lindsay stopped Lauren to talk.

"Lauren, my friend, whatcha' need to fix that pail

is a little honeybee honey," she said.

Lindsay took the pail and smeared honey over

the holes in the bottom. "Here ya go!" said Lindsay.

Lauren headed down the long path to the lake

with her sticky pail. When she returned to the

garden, only a few trickles of water came out.

Honey

The honeybee honey didn't help.

*N*ext, Anthony offered to help.

"A little Super Balooga fixes anything!" he said.

Anthony grabbed the pail and smooshed

bubblegum onto the bottom.

"You sure that's gonna work?" Lauren asked.

"Sure it will!" said Anthony.

Lauren took her pail and headed down the path to the

lake to fill her pail. When she finally returned to the

garden, she had only a little water left in her pail... again!

The Super Balooga didn't help.

Later that day, Madeline saw Lauren and called her over. "Never found a leak anywhere that a little "duck" tape couldn't fix!" Madeline bragged. She grabbed the pail from Lauren and quickly wrapped some strips of tape around the pail and handed it back.

Once more, Lauren filled her pail and headed up the path, splashing and sloshing water as usual. Along the way, the tape became soaked, and most of the water leaked out, same as it had always done.

The "duck tape" didn't help either.

Week after week, Lauren carried her pail up the long, winding path to the lake and back, splashing and leaking water all along the way. Lauren just kept on hoping and praying her hard work would make her seeds grow.

But, no matter how hard Lauren worked, it didn't help. Finally, one day as she looked down at the place where her brussel sprouts were supposed to be growing, tears started flowing down her cheeks.

"I'll never win anything... Ever!" she said.

Lauren's mother met her at the door.

"Momma, I've watered my brussel sprouts everyday, but it's not enough to make them grow!" she said.

Mother held Lauren tight. "My precious, little one, it was your job to water the seeds, but it's God's job to make things grow. Let's wait and see what He does with all of your hard work."

Lauren decided to stop worrying about her seeds.

She spent her time helping the other kids with their gardens.

On the day of the festival, Lauren heard someone calling her name.

"Lauren, come quick! Look what you've done!" Rachel yelled.

Beautiful wildflowers had bloomed along Lauren's path.

"How did this happen?" Lauren asked.

"You never gave up on your leaky pail,

and God never gave up on you!" Rachel replied.

At the festival celebration, Lauren's wildflowers won first prize. Everyone shouted, "Hooray for Lauren and her leaky pail!" The first place ribbon, and a shiny, gold trophy were placed at the table in front of her.

Lauren thanked everyone for the ribbon, but she told them they could keep the trophy...

...because, she already had one.

$\mathcal{L}$et us not become weary in doing good, for at the proper time we will reap a harvest if we do not give up. —*Gal 6:9*

The Land of Paddywhack Lane®

tower mountain

tall tree forest

sunshine garden

costume clubhouse

cuddles pet place

PETS